Valerie Carey

HARRIET AND WILLIAM AND THE TERRIBLE CREATURE

illustrated by Lynne Cherry

Beaver Books

A Beaver Book
Published by Arrow Books Limited
62-5 Chandos Place, London WC2N 4NW
An imprint of Century Hutchinson Ltd

London Melbourne Sydney Auckland
Johannesburg and agencies throughout the world

First published by Andersen Press 1985

Beaver edition 1987

Text © Valerie Carey 1985
Illustrations © Lynne Cherry 1985

Printed in Italy by Grafiche AZ, Verona

ISBN 0 09 943690 6

to my husband, Brent,
and my children, Kimberly, Allison and Jeffrey,
with love
V. S. C.

to my friends
at the Princeton Center
for Energy and Environmental Studies
L. C.

Harriet and William were twins. Harriet liked travelling. William liked working in his garden.

Harriet liked wearing new clothes. William liked wearing soft old clothes.

Harriet liked peanut butter sandwiches with jam. She liked ketchup with her scrambled eggs. William ate plain peanut butter, and he did not like ketchup.

The day Harriet finished building her spaceship, she said, "Let's go on a trip."

"No, thank you," said William.

"Why not?" asked Harriet.

"Because I could not sleep in a spaceship. I can only sleep in my own bed."

"You can't take your bed with you. It's a very small ship," said Harriet. "But you can take your pillow. Now will you come?"

"No," said William.

"Why not?" asked Harriet.

"I would rather stay home and take care of my garden," William said.

"All right," said Harriet. "Good-bye for now."

Va-ROOM went the spaceship. It took off into the sky with Harriet alone inside. Harriet was pushed against her seat as the spaceship went faster and faster.

"I wish William had come," she said to herself.

She passed the moon and all the planets.

Time for some exercise, thought Harriet. She was just unbuckling her seat belt when—

Crash!

Crump-a-bump.

The spaceship had landed. Harriet climbed out.

"Rocks and stumps. Stumps and lumps," she said. "William would not like this at all."

Crunch.

Harriet jumped.

Crunch and *munch.*

Harriet hid behind a rock.

Crunch. Munch. Smunch.

Harriet peeped around the rock. There was a TERRIBLE CREATURE, a dragonish thing. It had buggly eyes, a big snorting nose, and two webbed wings. And it had a mouth full of rocks. It was chewing rocks up. It was spitting rocks out.

"Oh my. Oh me," cried the creature. Big tears fell from its buggly eyes.

Harriet felt sorry for it. Even dragonish things must have feelings, she thought.

"Why are you crying?" she asked.

"You would cry too if you had to eat rocks," it said.

"Then why do you eat them?"

"Because all the flowers are gone. I ate them all. Then I ate all the trees. Now I am eating rocks because there is nothing else."

"Would you eat a Harriet if you saw one?" asked Harriet.

"Is a Harriet a flower, a tree, or a rock?" asked the creature.

"None of those," said Harriet.

"Then I would not eat one."

"Good," said Harriet, and she came out from behind the rock.

"Why don't you grow some flowers?" she asked.

"I don't know how," sobbed the creature. Big tears spattered on the rocks. Harriet handed it her handkerchief.

"I have an idea," she said. "I will help you if you will help me."

Harriet showed the creature her spaceship. "If I can just get it to fly again, I can go home and see my brother, William. He knows all about growing flowers. I am sure he would know what to do."

"I would like to help you, but I don't know anything about spaceships." The creature began to cry again.

"Don't worry about that." Harriet patted the creature, then got out her tools, and went to work.

At last she called the dragonish thing over. "Get behind the ship and blow as hard as you can. Just be careful not to blow fire."

The thing sucked in a big breath and *poof* let it out. Nothing happened. It sucked in a bigger breath. *Va-ROOM.* The ship lifted off the ground and into space.

Squish. The ship landed on William's tomatoes.
"They will never be the same," said William,
"but I am glad you are safe at home. I missed you."
Harriet hugged William. "I missed you, too."

She told him all about her trip and the dragonish thing. "William, will you please help?"

William frowned.

"Just this once, couldn't you please come along? You know so much more about planting gardens than I do."

William thought about leaving his garden with no one to take care of it. He thought about Harriet going alone. What if her spaceship crashed again? She could be stuck forever on that lumpy planet, with nothing to eat but rocks.

"I'll go," said William.

Harriet repaired her ship. William collected his garden tools and seeds.

"Snapdragon seeds should be good for a dragonish thing," he said.

"Don't forget sweet william," said Harriet.

William blushed.

"Do you have any Harriet flowers?"

"No," said William, "but you can take these. They are forget-me-nots."

"Thank you," said Harriet.

Harriet and William flew past the moon and all the planets. Harriet steered the ship straight to the terrible creature's home.

"I was afraid you would not come," it said.

"A promise is a promise," said Harriet.

The three worked hard to make a garden. William knew just what to do. They carried away rocks. They dug a well for water. They shovelled and raked the ground to make a flower bed.

At last the garden was planted.

"Thank you," said the terrible creature, and it began to cry.

"Why are you crying now?" asked Harriet. "Did we forget something?"

"No," sniffled the creature. "But now you will be going home, and I will miss you."

"Please don't cry," said William. "We will come again."

Harriet was proud of her brother. "I'm glad you said that. Travelling is not really so bad, is it?"

But William did not answer.

"What are you doing?" asked William one day.

"I am building a boat," said Harriet. "I am going to sail around the world. Will you come with me?"

"No, thank you," said William, and he went on weeding his garden.

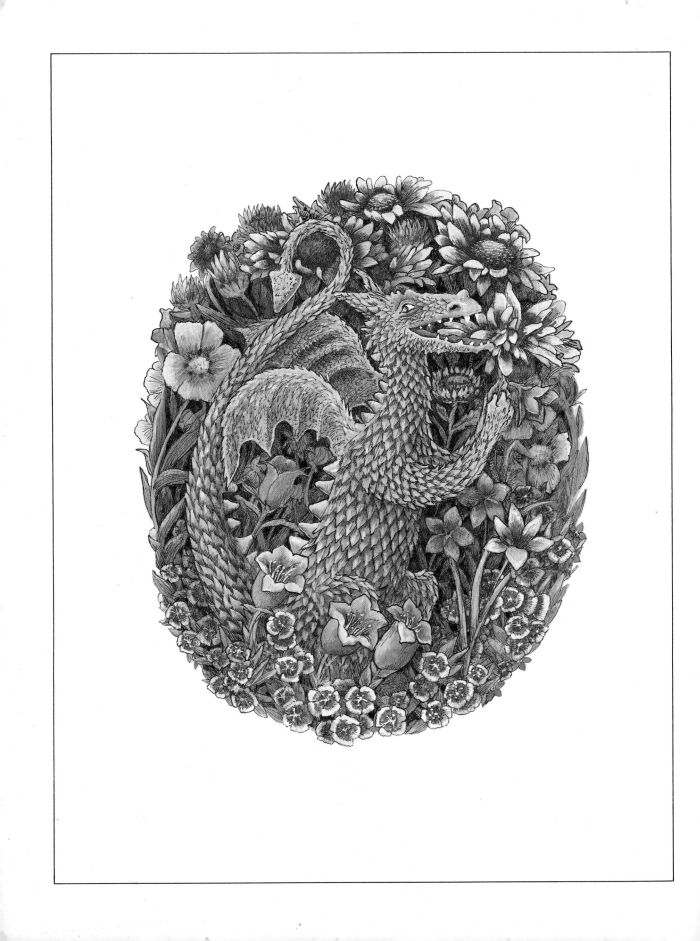